Mouse and Mole: The Secret of Happiness.
Published by Graffeg in 2021. Copyright ©
Graffeg Limited 2021.

Text copyright © Joyce Dunbar. Illustrations
copyright © James Mayhew. Design and
production Graffeg Limited. This publication
and content is protected by copyright © 2021.

Joyce Dunbar and James Mayhew are hereby
identified as the authors of this work in
accordance with section 77 of the Copyrights,
Designs and Patents Act 1988.

A CIP Catalogue record for this book is
available from the British Library.

ISBN 9781913134839

1 2 3 4 5 6 7 8 9

# MOUSE & MOLE
## The Secret of Happiness
### Joyce Dunbar and James Mayhew

This book belongs to:

_____

_____

_____

GRAFFEG

To my brilliant friend Magdalen Russell, with love from Mouse and Mole

For Caroline, Anthony, Connie and Arthur Clarke
With love, J. M.

# Contents

# A Good Read

Mouse sat down in his armchair with his book. So did Mole.
'There's nothing I like better than a good read,' said Mouse.
'Me too,' said Mole.

Soon Mouse was chuckling away. 'Ha! Ha-ha-ha-ha-ha!'

But Mole couldn't settle. He sat with his legs over one arm of the chair. Then he sat with his legs over the other.

'Ho-ho-ho-ho!' went Mouse, over his book.

Mole gave a deep sigh.

'Please stop fidgeting, Mole,' said Mouse, 'I am trying to read my book.'

'I am trying to read my book too,' said Mole, 'but I can't get comfortable.'

'Try plumping your cushion,' said Mouse.

Mole put down his book and stood up. He picked up his cushion and shook it. He threw down his cushion and thumped it. He put the cushion back in its place and patted it. Then he sat down again.

'Tee-hee-hee!' went Mouse.
Mole gave a very loud hiccup.
'What is it now?' asked Mouse.
'I've got hiccups,' said Mole.
'Try holding your breath,' said Mouse.

So Mole held his breath. He held it till he thought he was bursting. Then he gave a great gasp.

'What are you trying to do to me, Mouse?' he asked.

'I'm not trying to do anything to you,' said Mouse. 'I'm just trying to read my book.'

'But I've still – *hic* – got hiccups!' said Mole.

'Well, you could try pinching your snout and drinking a glass of water upside down.'

'Will you bring me a glass of water, please, Mouse?' asked Mole.

So Mouse brought Mole a glass of water and Mole tried pinching his snout and drinking it upside down. '*Hic!*' he went when he had finished.

'It didn't work,' he grumbled.
'What you need is a fright,' said Mouse.
'How do I get a fright?' asked Mole.

'LIKE THIS!' roared Mouse, jumping up at Mole.

'Oh, Mouse! You made me jump!' said Mole.

'Did I?' said Mouse. 'And how are the hiccups?'

Mole thought for a moment. Then he smiled. 'Gone,' he said. 'They've gone.'

'Good,' said Mouse. 'Now we can have a good read.'

'Ho-ho! Ha-ha!' went Mouse, after a while.
But Mole had started fidgeting again.

He wriggled and writhed and squirmed.
'What is it now?' asked Mouse.
'Now I have an itch,' said Mole.
'Scratch it then,' said Mouse.

'It's just in a place where I can't reach it,' said Mole. 'Right in the middle of my back. Will you scratch it for me, Mouse?'

Mouse sighed and put down his book. He began to scratch Mole's back.

'Higher, higher,' said Mole.

'Is that it?' said Mouse.

'Lower, lower,' said Mole.

'How's that?' said Mouse.

'Now you are tickling,' said Mole. 'Oh! Stoppit, Mouse, stoppit!'

So Mouse stopped scratching Mole's back and slumped down in his armchair.

Mole slumped down in his. Then Mole yawned, very loudly.

Mouse couldn't help yawning too.

Mole yawned again.

So did Mouse.

Then Mole said, through his yawn, 'That book you are reading looks very interesting, Mouse.'

'This book I am trying to read,' said Mouse.

'Oh, only trying?' said Mole. 'Why don't I read it for you? You never know. If we swap books it might stop me fidgeting and hiccuping and yawning.'

So Mouse and Mole swapped books. Then they both settled down for a good read.

'Ho-ho-ho!' chuckled Mole, after a while. 'Ha-ha-ha!'

But Mouse had started to fidget.

'Please stop fidgeting, Mouse,' said Mole, 'I am trying to read my book.'

# This Way and That

One morning, Mole made an announcement.

'Mouse! I am going for a walk!'

'What sort of walk?' asked Mouse.

'Just a walk.'

'Where to?' asked Mouse.

'This way and that,' said Mole. 'That way and this.'

'In that case,' said Mouse, 'could you please call on Owl and ask if he has a feather to spare?'

'All right,' said Mole.

Mole walked through the wood, straight to Owl's tree.

'Owl,' he called, 'Mouse wants to know if you have a feather to spare?'

'Sure,' said Owl, and a feather came floating down.

'There you are,' said Mole when he reached home. 'A feather from Owl. Now I am going on my walk.'

'On your way,' said Mouse, 'do you think you could call on Hedgehog and ask if he has a prickle to spare?'

'All right,' said Mole.

Mole went through the fields, straight
to the hedge where Hedgehog lived.

'Hedgehog,' he called out, 'Mouse
wants to know if you have a
prickle to spare?'

'I don't think I'd miss one,'
said Hedgehog, giving a
prickle to Mole.

'There you are,' said Mole
when he reached home.
'A prickle from hedgehog.
Now I am going on my
walk.'

'On your way,' said Mouse,
'would you mind calling on
Rabbit and asking if he has
a whisker to spare?'

'Oh, all right,' sighed Mole.

Mole went along to the grassy bank, straight to Rabbit's burrow. 'Rabbit,' he called, 'Mouse wants to know whether you have a whisker to spare?'

'Certainly not!' said Rabbit.

Mole went all the way back home. 'Rabbit says, "Certainly not!"' said Mole. 'And now I am going for my walk.'

'On your way—' began Mouse.

'Certainly not!' snapped Mole. 'MOUSE, I AM GOING FOR A WALK!'

'But you have been for three walks already,' said Mouse.

'Not that sort of walk,' said Mole. 'What I want is a carefree sort of walk. A happy-go-lucky sort of walk. You turned them all into ERRANDS!'

'But I thought it would make your walk useful,' said Mouse.

'I don't want a useful walk, I want a useless walk. I want a pointless walk. A walking-for-the-sake-of-it walk,' said Mole.

'What is the point of a pointless walk?' asked Mouse.

'And WHAT is the point, may I ask, of a feather from Owl, a prickle from Hedgehog, and a whisker from Rabbit?'

'Oh, none at all,' said Mouse.

'Then why did you ask for them?' asked Mole.

'Why, to give a point to your walk, of course,' said Mouse.

'Mouse! I am going for a walk,' said Mole. 'You have given a point to my walk. It is a slam-the-door-and-walk-off sort of walk!' And Mole slammed the door and walked off.

Mouse sighed. How difficult Mole could be.

# The Secret of Happiness

The light pepped in through the curtains. Day was beginning to dawn. Suddenly, Mole woke up.

'Mouse! Mouse! Wake up!' he cried.

'I have,' said Mouse, nearly jumping out of his skin. 'I am.'

'I had a dream,' said Mole.

'So did I,' said Mouse. 'Now can I go back and finish it?'

'But, Mouse! You don't understand. I dreamt that I knew the secret of happiness!'

'The secret of happiness is a good night's sleep,' grumbled Mouse.

'No, Mouse. You must listen. I really did dream that I had found the secret of happiness. And it was so obvious, as if I'd always known it.'

'Tell me after breakfast,' said Mouse.

'I can't,' wailed Mole. 'I've forgotten it!'

'Go back to sleep,' said Mouse. 'Then you might dream it again.'

'And I might not,' said Mole. 'I might forget that I ever dreamt it at all.'

'Well, we may as well have breakfast,' said Mouse, giving up and putting on his dressing gown.

Mole put on his dressing gown too, scratching his head all the while, trying to remember his dream.

'Was it a pair of warm slippers?' asked Mouse, putting on his own warm slippers.

'No, it wasn't,' said Mole.

'Perhaps it was a nice cup of tea,' said Mouse, putting on the kettle.

'No, it wasn't,' said Mole.

'Perhaps it was early-morning birdsong,' said Mouse, opening a window wide.

'No, it wasn't,' said Mole. 'It was none of these things. It sort of bubbled up, it sort of billowed, it sort of bloomed, from somewhere deep inside me. And it was so easy, Mouse, so easy in the dream.'

All day long Mole prowled around, scratching his head, trying to remember what it was. He was still scratching when Rat turned up for tea, with Hedgehog and Rabbit close behind.

'What's up, Mole?' asked Rat.

'I found the best thing in the world and I lost it,' burbled Mole. 'I shan't be happy again till I find it.'

'Mole's always losing things,' said Hedgehog.
'What is it this time?' asked Rabbit.
Mouse tried to explain.

Rat had an idea. 'I know how to help him to find it,' he
said. 'We must all try to jog his memory. Now, Mole, what
in the world would make you happy?'

'Well...' said Mole, looking
thoughtfully at Rat's hat.
'How about this four-leaf
clover I found?' said Hedgehog.
'It's sure to bring you lots
of luck.'
'Why, thank you, Hedgehog,'
said Mole.

'And I've brought a summer
pudding to share,' said Rabbit.
'You can have the biggest
helping.'
'Why, thank you, Rabbit,'
said Mole.

'And I promise you a ride on my
bicycle!' said Rat.
'Oh, I couldn't,' protested
Mole. 'But I have always liked
your green hat.'
'All right then, Mole. Here
you are. My one and only green
hat. Love it dearly.'

'Anything else?' asked Mouse.

'I wouldn't mind a stool for my feet and a cushion for my back,' said Mole.

'Whatever you want, Mole,' they all fussed. 'Your wish is our command.'

Before long, there sat Mole, his feet on a stool, his back on a cushion, his stomach full of summer pudding. 'Mmmmm,' he sighed, patting his hat, twirling his four-leaf clover. 'Mmmmm...'

Then, suddenly, it came: it sort of billowed, it sort of blossomed, it sort of bubbled up from somewhere deep inside him. A feeling of complete happiness. A smile spread over his face. 'I've got it!' he said. 'I've got it!'

'Well?' said his friends.

'The secret of happiness is...' Mole began.

'Yes?' said his friends.

'...is...izz...izzzzzzzzz,' went Mole.

But before he could say what it was, he fell into a deep, happy sleep.